Verge 2021

Verge 2021

Home

Edited by
Jessica Phillips, Anders Villani and Georgia White

MONASH
UNIVERSITY
PUBLISHING

Verge 2021: Home
© Copyright 2021

Monash University Publishing
Matheson Library Annexe
40 Exhibition Walk
Monash University
Clayton, Victoria 3800, Australia
publishing.monash.edu/

Monash University Publishing brings to the world publications which advance the best traditions of humane and enlightened thought.

ISSN: 2208-5637

ISBN: 9781922464439 (paperback)
ISBN: 9781922464446 (pdf)
ISBN: 9781922464453 (epub)

Design: Les Thomas
Typesetting: Jo Mullins

Cover image: © Maya Irving, 2021, *The Lamp Was Low and Golden*. Used with kind permission from the artist.

A catalogue record for this book is available from the National Library of Australia.

Contents

Acknowledgements

As editors, we would like to begin by acknowledging the people of the Kulin nation as the Traditional Custodians of the land on which *Verge* is produced. Sovereignty was never ceded, and it is our privilege to be able to live, work and learn here. We extend our deepest respects to Elders past, present and emerging, and we acknowledge the rich history of storytelling embedded in the cultures of Aboriginal and Torres Strait Islander peoples.

Our thanks goes out to Dr John Hawke for his assistance with coordinating the *Verge* editorial team and for his critical expertise as our peer reviewer. We would also like to thank Joanne Mullins and the team at Monash University Press for the time and effort they put towards making this publication possible, and to the students, staff, and members of faculty at the School of Languages, Literatures, Cultures & Linguistics at Monash University who provided editorial guidance and assisted with our calls for submissions:

Rebecca Bryson
Dr Melinda Harvey
Dr Chris Murray
Sally Riley

Last but not least, our sincere thanks to all contributors and to everyone who submitted work for consideration in *Verge*. We were privileged to read so many brilliant and thoughtful pieces, all of which brought some much-needed warmth to what was a very 'unhomely' year.

Jessica Phillips, Anders Villani and Georgia White

Foreword

For all the suffering it has wrought, the COVID-19 pandemic has also profoundly altered the rhythms by which we live. In the most optimistic sense, such an alteration carries with it a kind of latitude: a rare opportunity to take stock of experiences we have been too enveloped and swept along by to fully apprehend. As the Polish author Olga Tokarczuk puts it, the isolation that most of us have endured 'has raised a question we have rarely had the courage to ask ourselves: what is it, exactly, that we keep going off in search of?'

It seemed necessary, then, to theme this edition of Monash University's Creative Writing anthology 'Home'. Recognition follows lack: deprived of so much that feels intimate, familiar, communal, easeful, we engage with these states of thinking and feeling as perhaps never before. A vital method of that engagement, of course, is art, given its power to elicit compassion, and to bridge the public and private spheres. The pieces you are about to read, chosen from an outstanding crop of submissions, voice the theme in styles, details, and attitudes that are as wildly disparate as they are coherent: a Chinese student living in Sydney battles the distances of geography and racial stigma; a *Kardiya* (white) woman examines the terms of connection in a remote Indigenous community; a successful life consists of joining a queue of unknown length, leading to an unknown future.

What we have endeavoured to do as editors is let the work speak for itself. We believe it speaks richly to the present moment.

Jessica Phillips, Anders Villani and Georgia White

1

Pretty Little Thing

Rowan Heath

Little catches the bloody feathers as they drift to the floor. The bird pokes them through the bars one by one, clearing the bottom of her cage until all that's left is a bustle of straw and white shit. She takes a moment to examine her work, then claws back up to her perch to tear more feathers from her back, contorting like a broken thing, chittering like an angry one. The ferocious way she hacks at her skin, the pink, puckered flesh now red, holds me still and quiet.

Little bends to snatch fluff from the air. She cradles her haul in her palms, a blue-white mist speckled with crimson. I want to smack her knuckles and force the feathers out of her hands.

Little came home one day with a fresh pair of eyes. She saw our old house in new ways. She crept along new paths between rooms, sticking close to the walls, placing silent footfalls along parts of the floor we rarely touched. She slowed at every doorway, peered around every corner. She scanned the furniture, noting every crinkle, crease, and shadow, as if everything had been switched while she was at school. If I tried to mimic her, I had to flatten myself along the wall like an oversized, awkward starfish, my chin and chest getting in the way. I stubbed my toes on the skirting while she seemed to float along it like a cat on a fence.

Little demonstrated a newfound ability for shrinking. She could fold herself down to almost nothing, crumple so that she barely fit into her clothes. We caught her under beds, tucked into closets, wedged in the space between the toilet bowl and the wall. She hid from Mum, from me, from no one. I remember one night hearing a screech from the bathroom, full-throated and bloody. Mum almost stepped on Little while she hid at the bottom of the shower, peering up at her like a child-ghost. Mum took her by the scruff of the neck and dragged her back to her room. I watched them grapple in silence from the other end of the hall. Mum was about to walk out when something changed her mind. She saw me watching, and an expression came over her face that I still don't understand. She shut the door. The two of them were in there for a long time, and they were both very quiet.

The bird brought Little back. She stood by the wall of the lounge room one afternoon clutching a cardboard box, the creature chittering away inside. She didn't engage with it at all – it might as well have been an empty box. Her eyes flicked from one place to another: the door leading to the kitchen, the looming bookshelf, the open window. But once the pretty cage was assembled and the box emptied, the bird had all her attention. It sprung up onto the rocky perch and shivered as if shaking off water. Its snowy head snapped about as if to take us all in, and no matter which way it sat, it always had an eye on us.

For the first few moments Little simply watched the bird, her focus so complete that she was still for the first time in weeks. Mum stood nearby, stiff-backed, as if waiting for Little to turn away and slip behind the curtains, or creep along the walls, or wedge herself under the couch.

Little began to coo. I remember it as a gentle, almost inaudible sound, barely louder than an exhale. The bird tilted its head and hopped along the perch. Little pursed her lips to make kissy sounds at it, and soft little clicks at the back of her throat. Eventually those coos and clicks turned into elongated sounds, and those sounds became words, ephemeral and meaningless.

Mum crept towards Little and whispered into her ear, 'Pretty little bird,' as if asking a question. Little took on the words unconsciously, forming them in her mouth, ringing them out like tiny bells. She repeated them in her softest voice, over and over, adjusting her emphasis from one syllable to the next. Mum stepped back and sank onto the couch.

I remember wanting to ask a question, but when I opened my mouth no sound came out. I was spellbound, I couldn't speak. It was as though someone was holding me tight while saying: 'Hush, hush, hush.'

'Shame,' she muses. 'Pretty little thing. Even with the growth.'

Birds get tumours in old age. We both know this. The vet told us that nothing worthwhile could be done. I found little to grieve about in that, though I felt the horrible weight of responsibility shifting onto me.

'You should've named it, it's yours,' I say to Little. She cocks her head and frowns at the bird, as if it's a puzzle she's struggling to decipher. She presses the feathers in her hands. Some are stuck together with gore.

'You should've named it,' I repeat.

'How should I do it then?' Her voice is empty. She studies the feathers as she packs them down with her thumbs.

'You don't have to.' I don't want this to be my problem.

'That's what you're saying, though, right? My bird.'

'No, that's not what I mean.'

'You want me to hit it with a brick? Lock it in the freezer? Put it in a plastic bag and suck the air out myself? You fucking do it.'

She drops the clump of feathers and leaves. The bird doesn't care that Little is gone. She doesn't see me. She hacks at herself as if on instinct. If she weren't moving so much I'm sure I'd see that her eyes were glazed over.

Little at this age is very tempered in her anger. She doesn't stomp, she doesn't yell, she doesn't slam doors. She doesn't rage out loud. She's difficult to argue with because she never bites back.

I follow Little to her room. I'm young. I want to snap. I want her to give me a reason to explode. I lean on the doorframe and cross my arms over my chest.

'I thought you'd care more. You used to love that bird.'

Little ignores me, busying herself at her desk. Her bony shoulders are strung high, and in the tiny crease between her eyebrows I see a quickening flame. I push on.

'It used to mean everything to you. You loved it more than Mum.'

'I don't care. I don't remember.'

'I do. I remember the day we got it. It was love at first sight. You even used to have conversations with it.' Little picks up a book, but her knuckles are white. 'That bird was the only thing you talked to for like, three months or something. After that thing happened at school. You had your own little bird language. It was adorable.'

Little turns her eyes on me. I want her face to be a white, volcanic rage boiling over, but I see something unexpected. Confusion. Apprehension. She's at a loss, and the hot, drunken pride welling in my chest drains in an instant.

'What thing?' Her voice is very quiet.

'You don't remember?'

'Tell me.'

The hollow space in my stomach lets me know, somehow, that I've done something I'll come to regret. Yet if I were to be silent, I'd be denying her something she is owed. A seriousness takes hold of me as I tell her all the things she doesn't know about herself. How she came home one day a different creature. How she crept along the walls and didn't speak, how she frightened Mum in the shower. How she did all sorts of strange things like hiding in cupboards, sleeping under beds instead of in them, and scratching her thighs red raw. I tell her about the months when she stopped playing all games but hide and seek, that she was always the hider, and that if I found her on accident she would screech as if she were being flayed alive, and each time it happened it took a whole night to calm her down.

Little listens in silence. As I run out of stories, I find my voice wilting to a whisper. Her face grows stark, and all at once a wave of horror and understanding tumbles over her. She jumps to her feet and pushes me out of the room so hard I almost fall.

When Mum comes home, I confess with the bitter tears of a criminal. I don't fully understand why. She sends me to bed and spends the rest of the night coaxing her way into Little's room with whispers and coos.

It's been a while since I've seen her this thin. The last time I visited home, Little was – what, fifty-five kilos, at least. Now she's a wisp of a thing. Taller than me, but lighter. I want to scoop her up, I want to yell at her. I know I could do both, so I choose to be silent.

'You coming in?' She holds the door so that there's no room for me to pass. Or, maybe, so that the rain doesn't come in with me. I step forward, and the door swings open, making space. Little heads back up through the house.

She sits by the counter. I ask her what she's reading and she doesn't respond. I study her profile, the wispy hairs curling on the back of her neck, the pasty tint in her skin, the troughs beneath her eyes. I feel as though I can hear every individual raindrop splatter on the roof.

I rehearse some conversation starters as we sit in silence. How is school? What did you do last weekend? The silence rolls on and these questions mutate, swelling into beasts that prowl on the edge of my tongue. I want to set them free. I want to ask her why we don't talk anymore. I want to know if she misses me.

Little is barricaded in misery. It's in her eyes and the slope of her shoulders. She's this way for one reason. For a million reasons. Likely because of me.

The rain falls in a grey blur. The past is very present today. It colours me like a blush. I think of the bird Little had a long time ago, that she treated like a part of herself and slowly forgot. Its skeleton lies beneath the shivering plum tree.

I don't think I processed its death properly. I don't feel bad about the act itself, not in the way that I should. When I held the bird, I wasn't thinking of mercy. It was warm and squirming and soft. I counted in time with the drum roll of its heartbeat against my thumb. If I hesitated, it was because I was comforted by how alive it felt in my hands.

I did it for the wrong reasons. I didn't care about putting the thing out of its misery. Killing the bird was about me, about my guilt. I wanted the act to stain me.

No one knows the bird is there under the plum tree. Mum and Little never asked me about it. I don't know what they think.

We've been quiet for so long it feels wrong to speak. But I say something meaningless about the storm, and Little nods, her dull eyes fixed on the page.

When we speak it's like we're having two conversations at once. One made up of things we say that don't really matter, and another, parallel conversation made up of things we don't say, that do matter. If I ask her about the weather, it's because I can't ask her if she forgives me. And when she answers, even in silence, I don't absorb her answer. Instead, I hear her voice in the conversation we're not having, demanding: 'What did you do to my bird?'

A thunderclap splits over our heads. Little stands up as if she can't bear to sit any longer. I see two versions of her walk to the front door. There's the Little of now, sixteen, taller than me but thinner, stepping light-footed down the hallway and peeling her socks off. Behind her creeps the Little I remember from years ago. She tiptoes down the house, pausing at every open door, peering back over her shoulder. This Little darts into a shadowy corner, disappearing as the older one steps out into the wailing gale.

'You coming?'

I follow her outside. She is drenched already, smaller now that her clothes are wet. She tells me to take off my shoes.

'Why?'

'Just do it.'

I stand by the door barefoot. I tell myself that I owe her. Yes, I owe her this and everything.

'What are we doing?'

She looks at me over her shoulder, her expression unreadable. We have a short, inaudible conversation. With a gesture she invites me to follow her into the rain.

In the conversation we don't have, the one that matters, I stop her there and ask, 'Why do you want me here?'

She skids down the rain-slicked driveway. The road bubbles and shimmers like a black brook, choked on both sides by grey water rushing into the storm drains. Little plunges her naked feet into the churning gutter.

The water is swollen with debris: rocks, garbage, gum leaves. It's a living thing, moving against me, billowing out at my ankles. Little moves to the middle of the road and I stay in the gutter, stones cutting into the soles of my feet.

The streetlights are on, though it isn't dark enough for them yet. Far off, near the horizon, black clouds catch fire. Little looks directly above at the tumult of the storm and waits. I want to ask her a question but I can't speak. It's as though someone is holding me tight and whispering in my ear: 'Hush, hush, listen.'

A jagged, white crack appears in the sky, striking the ground just beyond our suburb. The whole world holds its breath and I with it, suspended in the static, empty moment before the thunderclap. Another white burst cleans out the sky, and a moment later the thunder comes, shaking the world between two hands.

Little has her mouth open. Her nose is curled towards her eyebrows and her eyes are shut tight. I can't separate her voice from the thunder, and I can't make out what she's saying.

She may be screaming. She may be simulating a scream. She may have brought the thunder herself with the same magic the bird used to bring her voice back.

I want to weep all of a sudden. I want to sob out loud. I wish I was the type to cry.

I remember the night Little showed me what her teacher had shown her, moving her hands up her legs, pinching the skin until it flushed bright red. I watch her and wonder how anyone could do something so horrible to somebody else.

In the conversation we're not having, Little's voice merges with the storm and drowns me in its questions.

Why did it happen?

Why did you tell her?

What did you do with the bird?

She closes her mouth and the world grows still. How empty the street feels when it's quiet. The rain presses down in one great rush as if the storm, suspended for a moment, has only paused to take a breath before raging on.

Little inhales, heaving her chest to the sky. She turns to me and I see something I don't expect. She's flushed, plump, animated. Blown up with cartoonish warmth, as if the distance between us were a layer of dirt that could be washed away. She holds out her hand and my heart recoils. I don't know how to take it. I don't have the right.

She presses her palm against mine anyway, and pulls me to the centre of the street. I experience the strange, impossible sensation of having moved uphill.

The sky bursts. Little taps my shoulder as she counts down to the thunder. Her touch is like permission, a hammer breaking through a wall I could never get through alone. Three taps is all it takes to banish the voice that bids me hush. The firm arms wrapped around me unravel.

I open my mouth and it all tumbles out. The sound I make is like a thunderclap. I'm not myself for a moment. I'm not here, I'm not anywhere. I'm just a sound, whirling in a void, revelling in my magnitude.

Her hand stays on my shoulder in the silence that comes after. She has enough rain magic for us both. For a few seconds we're all that's left of the living world. It's just us, the faint, burbling gutters, the streetlights, and the storm.

We go home when our voices are hoarse and the rain has seeped into our bones. We bring the storm into the house with us, so much of it that our footprints are muddled into one grainy trail.

Rainwater falls from Little's eyelashes, runs down her nose, and plummets from her chin. She wrings her hair out onto the carpet and shakes like a wet bird. Her cheeks are rosy, her eyes bright. I pant like I've been running. She pauses as if waiting for me to catch my breath. She's working something out, arranging her thoughts. She smiles, and it's like she's reading my mind.

'I think it's time we talked.'

2

Groaner, After Suicide

Gavin Yates

Ocean to hatched rhythm, feathering
an Auden diamond.

Such large white shadows, unstable
cliff edges.

A shovel of raspberries: blonde
and only conspicuous.

Copying staccato lacework for the wash
of cleared profile.

Never unscrewed. Stream, medicine,
probably: I have unlimited guesses.

Drink from the jar, turn spotlight
onto the street. The point is faint

with all rush, vapour—return once more,
one more try,

try a million times. The upshot is,
spinning wheel

scarcely a groove in the low particle.
Can't get my head around it.

3

Coming Home

Shalom Verghese

(Soft) sleep rests in the lanes of her neck.

She bathes in the waters
of her redemption,
waits for the neckties to wander
over her breast,
to linger across her lips
and disintegrate
across her ankles.

She waits for herself
to awaken,
like dust that pulls
moths into the ocean.
She waits for the emerging
to come,
for a boy in black with sheep ties
on his neck and lanes in his throat
to whisper death
not rebirth
but a flick of nickels
against her knuckles.

Like I flick nickels against my knuckles, not against my
flick, like I flick knuckles against my nickels, not against
my flick, not against my knuckles, but against my nickels
against my flick.

She unplugs the waters
redeems the wandering neckties
not against her ankles
but against the lips against the hipbones
pulls moths to awaken from the ocean
into dust not to emerge again in black
not with sheep ties from her throat
but the lanes from her throat.

And we melt under our clothes, a practised patterning.

Like I flick nickels against my knuckles, not against my
flick, like I flick knuckles against my nickels, not against
my flick, not against my knuckles, but against my nickels
against my flick.

4

The Ladle

Derek Chan

My grandmother mixes
minced pork, chives, crushed garlic, a pinch of
corn starch & sesame. I sift
silence, separate dough, watch flour
catch on her brow, imagining
younger eyes of a browner earth
burned years ago. She frowns,
takes my dough, glazes
the edges with water,
her ginger-rooted fingers
teasing out trapped air. I listen
to her wheeze & wonder
what stories have never been told,
what bodies lie buried
under the pale precipitate of her
breath; did the walls of her childhood
home ever smell of cassia bark
& ground galangal? She pulls
my apron tighter, tucks
the last wonton, brings the soup to simmer.
We wait. Our faces die-cast
in colander light. A salt-soft sound
I shift closer to catch: *Once, during winter...*
Then, the broth breaks into boil.

She hands me the ladle, dusts off
her mitts, lifts the lid.
The steam rising between us
like a memory.

5

Zuihitsu

Derek Chan

After Jenny Xie

Wake into toothache of alarm. The sun arrows itself in all directions, a lunatic compass. The sky does not remember itself here.

Outside, the city breathing its own exhalant, cars tracing maps over maps. Buildings stacked neat white like the mah-jong set in my aunt's closet. Through the coarse cloth of the clouds, a moon cleaves at my eye's capillaries. I wait for a new syntax to arrive.

At the Hung Hom wet markets, light hardens into the bright sharp of a beak. Crabs strangled in plastic bags. One tongue draped on another, stray eyeballs asking for a stranger's appetite. I swim through wet voices.

Fisherman pulling trawls of fish from the oily Sham Shui harbour. Deft hands parting organ from muscle. The infinite colours colliding inside a single scale. With enough tenacity, every layer can be eaten. Even the bones, the marrow.

Shopping for dragon-fruits with my uncle, whom I last saw when I was eight years old. *Too ripe, too firm.* The dark pits of his eyes, the stems of his veins. *What have they been teaching you over there?* The answers buried inside the soil of me. I close my eyes, focus on my touch, my feel.

Think about it, laughed the woman waiting in line ahead of me, *Chinatowns only really exist outside of China.*

My mother's old bedroom in Kwun Tong. Scent of sebum and dehydrated dream. Half-moons where fingertips lifted dust from the windowsill. Under the bed, rat droppings make an oasis for the flies. I make note of all this.

The self lives at the edge of its own border. A name that speaks itself alive. At the monastery, a Buddhist monk explains: *Do not mistake 'I am' for 'I am this.'*

Dentures drying by an open window. Tiger Balm hardened like duck fat on a cotton sleeve. In an unnamed village forty years away, frangipanis grow quietly through floorboards. How little the body leaves behind.

Dawn breaking open like a knife parting a mango. The mornings when my grandmother kneels on her prayer-mat, words swimming inside her lungs. Faith, too, can be a form of disbelief. She believes in nothing her hands will give her.

The brush-blur of train rides. Guangzhou, Pudong, Guiyang. My parents and I do not speak. Silence, too, can be an entrance: a nakedness the eyes cannot pry open. Outside, lights flutter like beads on the night's thread.

I listen to the pavements. Their patterns. Try to ignore the stench. During the war, people were buried in mortar craters across their streets. Cost-effective. After the war, there were too many bodies to recover. Cheaper to build over it.

Grief is a language I fail to untangle, a mouth with its own idea of an ending.

Here, now, in Australia. My mother by the kitchen sink, her tongue tracing ampersand after ampersand in the air before me. What shape is she trying to learn by *xīn* (heart)? What is *here, now* anyway? The repeating comma of her lips as she calls out to me: *My xīn. My xīn. My sin.*

Hiding in the attic when I was four. Trying to read sentences of dust under a strip of light. One story shifting into another.

A half-memory. After a nightmare, sweet soil of urine rising from the sheets. My father wiping the sweat from my back. His hands the smell of yew bark and coffee rinds. Three lines from Li Bo placed into the curve of my ear: *Zhuangzi dreamed of being a butterfly / Or perhaps the butterfly dreamed of being Zhuangzi / Which was real – the butterfly or the man?*

6

A Letter from the Bottom of a Well

Derek Chan

*My father's cousin suddenly disappeared during the mass-seizure movement of
the Cultural Revolution. His body was never found, and the exact reasons for his
disappearance were never confirmed. Rumours suggested he had either been killed
by Mao Zedong's soldiers or forced to flee the country. According to one story, he
had been drowned in a well.*

Mā ma, Mā ma, wǒ xī wàng nǐ shēn tǐ jiàn
kāng. Nǐ hái zài zhǎo wǒ ma? Bié hài pà, wǒ hěn kuài jiù
huì huí jiā / to rub fish oil into your back / & place a
glass / of warm jasmine by your bed side / don't worry
about me / down here / it is dark enough / to remember
the sound of azaleas opening / to the memory / of
daylight / down

here / nothing beautiful can grow / only
shattered & found / like the crushed wings of a swallow /
flickering in mud / or trumpet lilies wrapped around /
bones porcelain & iridescent / or perhaps these hands / I
cupped to my face / as a sign of forgetting / how the
body longs for / more than water / my brothers' faces /
floating up to meet me / in the broken bowl of

these palms / there is so much music / in
memory / so much memory / in music / the long nights /

when I played the strings of the rain / falling through my
fingers / & heard only of / my thirst for you / a dusk of
your voice / or was it the broken thrum ringing / from the
jaw of a dead bullfrog / the long nights / where I looked
up at the moon / mistaking it for the brightest exit / of a
gun

        chamber / the stars shot down / into teeth
rattling / across these salt-slicked stones / the moss I run
my lips across nightly / for the silk of a woman's thighs /
Mā ma! / Mā ma! / Wǒ hěn lěng! / Wǒ hěn lěng! / the
winters down here are so dark / when will it be Spring /
again the orchards ripening everywhere / daylight on the
tongue / sweet as strips of rice milk / everywhere
ripening the Spring /

        field 7.62mm rifle he cracked / against my
temple / his fists heavy / with the scent of freshly pulped
/ magnolias & burned stupas / the young soldier's eyes
ripening / like orchards / as our bodies bloomed / open
like orchards / in the serrated night of knees / dragged
through rust / & fresh semen / of wet cornfields / my
white palms / dangling ahead / like two lit windows /
they tossed me

        down / I didn't know why / the water knew
/ my name / why the water still speaks / my name / but
don't worry about me / down here / it is dark enough / to
remember the sound / of your voice opening / to the
daylight / of memory / down here / all water returns / to
the body it came from / the body where we will meet
again / & drink from what's left of mine

7

Manifesto

Anders Villani

Once, I gathered every leaf
I could find with a spider
egg sac grafted to it.

I burnt these leaves inside, on the stove,
how I'd seen my mother char
poblanos over an open flame.

Next, I found those parts
of myself that were white as gulls.
Lightless parts: underside of wrist,

etcetera.
I burnt these parts with an asthma inhaler
until scars rose

like dead fish to the surface
of all rivers. Not poisoned—
that was as specific as I wished to go

that day. Not poisoned. My brother's
mattress lay on cinderblocks
dusty enough to write on,

not dusty enough for that writing to be legible.
Here, I wrote my reasons.
I remember the wind chime
changing the wind.

8

Q

Anders Villani

Your housemate is in his room, almost touching a world
without government, military forces, or taxes. A lovely
guy, from overseas, from the country, who lives in the city now.

When the virus hit, he lost his income. He couldn't get JobKeeper.
He's out of tobacco—maybe you emptied his pouch—
which is fine, because it's just another adulterant.

Politics has never held the slightest interest for him.
Politics is like light, or poetry: it holds no interest until it does,
and then it's everywhere. Joe Rogan knows. But let's forget Joe.

Let's forget peer-review. Let's focus on this guy, too sweet
with plum vape, who as a child skinned mink and barrowed
remains to a skip among tall, snow-fleeced firs, birches—

he smokes the last pre-dawn joint pure, like the infinite
energy they're hiding. The cancer cures, the spacecraft. The black
Trumpers. The hurting of children how his mother was.

Try to parse your feelings for him. The night he came home
closer to friendless and held, contritely, that he'd be dead
before he saw Bill Gates's doctors; the night he had you examine

footage of the migrant caravan for the smart phones, the crisp
blue jeans, the blue wristbands actors flashed to get fed, paid—
on nights like these, how much did you write off?

Of all visions, utopia is the most fundamentally good
at taking everything. You write poems: you get it. You're meant to
be able to hate the white a person says, and love the yolk.

9

The Queue

Gemma Grant

If you want to make something of your life, you will join the queue. Sure, you will first try to make a go of it in the city, but that will only last you so long. You will tell yourself that you have more to offer than the rest of those poor sods who have already packed up and left. You may even nab an enviable position as an engineer or bank teller, or perhaps as a cleaner. A job like that will last you a few good months, but it will hardly cover the rent payments and you can't afford for your credit score to get any lower.

One evening, after a particularly dire day at the office, you will be driving home. You opt for the Eastern Freeway. You used to take a more direct course but these days it really isn't safe to venture far from the city's primary motorways. You thank your God (if you still have one) that this road is still fixed with security cameras and remembers the concept of criminal account-ability. At least here they still pretend to investigate the jackings.

As you hurtle along, contemplating the woes of personal responsibility and the oily smile of your landlord, you will be inexplicably moved by a large billboard glued to the sky. It is nothing more than bolded white text on a black background. It reads: *LET THE QUEUE WORK FOR YOU!* Although you have never noticed the sign before, today you can't help but consider its plea. It has caught you on a vulnerable day and has planted the idea in your belly. It doesn't take long to bloom.

And so try as you might to resist, you will eventually submit to the mag-netic pull of the queue. You will give your two weeks' notice (if you feel like it), pack up your house into a suitcase, sell the rest of your belongings (you won't need the relics of your city life where you're going), and dutifully take your place at the back of the line.

Congratulations! You have now set your family on the path to a promising future.

*

Agatha and I joined the queue about 150 klicks ago. We wanted to start a family and all the good schools are at the front of the line. It was the right time for us anyway. Agatha was an attorney in the city, but she hadn't been getting many clients since all the legislation expired. You see, they decided that it was good and modern to put expiration dates on all the written laws. That way, they would have to be updated to stay relevant and we would never run the risk of imposing outmoded, archaic regulations on our modern society. But then they all lapsed, and it was too much work for the Parliament to draft new ones. It was really a bit of an oversight looking back on it now.

In any case, this left Agatha without work. It wasn't long before she began to flirt with the idea of the queue. I would come home from the office and she would ambush me with statistics from the other side. She presented me with graphs boasting high employment rates, reasonable housing prices, extraordinary happiness index scores. It was all waiting for us at the front of the line, she said. And it was hard to say no to her. It was all so reasonable.

Since we joined the queue all that time ago, so many have followed that we can no longer see the end of it. The queue is a heaving serpent, always humming, animated by the anxious energy of its occupants. I suppose that's because although you could call it our primary residence, it is fundamentally a waiting place. When you join the queue, your natural state becomes one of anticipation. They say the restlessness dissipates when you reach the front but these days, I can't even imagine a version of myself who has nothing to wait for.

It is in poor taste to admit it, but there are some things that I'm going to miss about the queue once I'm spat out the other end. I am proud to report that we have a strong sense of community here. I suppose it's only natural, really. To act in the interest of your neighbour is to act for yourself.

Of course, it is your responsibility to establish yourself in the queue, but once you have earned the trust of your fellow queue-dweller, you can leave whenever you like. The queue is very reasonable. If you are affable and honest, we will hold your place for you.

About 45 klicks ago, poor Mrs. Gardiner had to surrender her place for a couple of weeks. Her back pain had become utterly incapacitating and she had to be carted off to the nearest hospital for corrective spinal surgery. Of course, I feel sorry for the old girl, but I will say that she did bring it upon herself – that flimsy fold-up garden chair of hers was hardly going to give her the support she needed. She insisted on keeping it because it 'reminded her of George' – but what good is sentimentality when you're bent double like an inverted capital L?

While she was away, we got rid of that horrid chair. Then we all chipped in and bought her one of those upholstered recliner lounges that you see in the infomercials. The queue is very community-minded.

Now, it is not always pleasant to discuss, but you should know that we have instituted a series of strict measures to deal with those who do not adhere to our core values. It is important to understand that not everyone is going to respect the community. They say that a few years ago, a young man jumped his place when the bloke in front of him had to go to the hospital to treat the gangrene in his leg. It was a deeply disturbing situation, but you will be relieved to learn that we have a zero-tolerance queue-jumping policy. As soon as the queue discovered the infraction, they dealt with it swiftly and cleanly. They say that once you reach the site where they buried him, you only have about 70 klicks to go until you reach the front of the queue. Agatha and I have a bottle of champagne ready for the occasion.

I don't know how long we have to go or where it will all end. Agatha says that they must have built the new civilisation in the desert, but I think it will be somewhere near the water. Sometimes if I close my eyes, I can hear the distant lapping of waves against a sunburnt shore. The sounds started faint, but I swear they're getting louder.

10

Is It the Same for You

Joan Fleming

There are days when the slowness makes me want to engineer a small harm, a neat puncture in the thigh, nothing permanent. My nephew tells me there is a banishment spell, but I haven't found the right tone for it. Not with this concrete month, daubs pushed around the same hung cardboard rectangle 'til crayon trips on the corrugation the going-over's torn through to. Tell me if you think it was cruel of me to have him wish out loud for a spell to make his legs run faster? The brace makes him unsteady on every crossing, on every rock, or does the brace help. The larger part of me today wants to cut a decent pain body from the climbing fig in the courtyard, but the neighbour I imagine stopping me with a stare from their window is what stops me from it. The scissors are a kindness, their sharpness, they don't understand. The smaller part of me hopes the fish will come apart in potting soil without giving off any kind of smell. The slow thing wrong with it was Ich or Fluke or the Marble Gene, but nothing I could see, nothing I knew what to do with. The things I see repeat as in a film a child watches over and over again, this may be why the days are two hours long. I know you plastered over the burgundy mess with a sand paste that reads as concrete, but all of that you chose, did you not? I was lying on my back to give the hands of the dead their natural receptiveness, and telling the square of sky between the two apartment blocks that it was my only nature. So we didn't see the green rest gasping, but who cares about that, I don't want you to feel bad about that. It's just a thing that happens when two directions remake each other. I want to say as well that it wasn't a bad thing that you talked all the way up the mountain, it's what most people do, and you've always been more used to hills, as you say, their camber and crouch and the screech of the promise of a summit, the getting-there, you didn't know a mountain had an inside, how could you. She isn't really spending a thousand a week on taxis to the hospital to re-up on short-acting hypnosis, it's a little more than that, or a little less, difficult to be exact unless you see the statements, tremendous to me still how the machine keeps perfect track. I wouldn't bother adding up. It'll only make you glue, something right for holding a shoe together, three months max, maybe four, though we can't go walking anyway. I don't understand how they don't keep records, or say no, but then again I never trained in that breed of insistence. I used to think limpid was a word meaning very slow. It floors me too, seeing the rocks right down at the bottom, the water somehow even more clarified than air. When she gave me the fish I worried it would die from something in the water, the water wrong, too clean or new or not new enough, an environment too lightly imbued with the fish itself, or not at all. It seemed sick when I cleaned the rocks and sick when I didn't, that's what kind of parent I would be, fretting the days in the treated water. I wrote to her today to say we love you, and travel safe, but I don't imagine she can receive even this without a minimum temperature of shame. But give it some time. I imagine poems will soon be written about all this in a language whose verb charts I once held out a hand for. You speak it though, and I want to say, you did everything you could. I want to tell you that, because it's true, and is it Spring that's doing it? Convoluting the city air with chirp, or is it because we've pulled all the doors in place. Almost daily I receive, as I know you do, the meetable and unmeetable lists of should. A long and warming blade we know is searching through the wood.

11

The Meetable and Unmeetable Lists of Should

Terry Craven

(Ongoing collaboration with Joan Fleming)

Is it the same for you

There are afternoons when the slowness makes me want to engineer a small puncture in the thigh, nothing permanent, a little pain. My nephew tells me there is already a spell to send things away, but I wouldn't have the right tone for it. Not with this olive month, yellow-green, the only flourish. Tell me if you think it was cruel of me to have him wish out loud for a spell to make his legs run faster? The brace makes him unsteady on every crossing, on every rock, or does the brace help. The largest part of me today wants to cut a decent pain body from the potted ficus in the courtyard, but the neighbour I imagine stopping me from their window stop me from it. The scissors are a kindness, their sharpness, they wouldn't understand. The smaller part of me hopes the fish will come apart in potting soil without giving off any kind of smell. It was Ich or Fluke or maybe the Marble Gene, but nothing I saw, nothing I could see. The things I see repeat as in a film a child watches over and over again, this may be why the days are two hours long, I know the warp made the weft read olive, but that was something you chose, did you not? I was lying on my back to give the hands of the dead their natural receptiveness, and telling the square of sky between the two apartment buildings that it was my only nature. So we didn't see the green come into it, but who cares about that, I don't want you to feel bad about that. It's just a thing that happens when two directions remake each other. I want to say as well that it wasn't a bad thing that you talked all the way up the mountain, it's what most peopl. . . ., and you've always been more used to lulls, as you said, their cambered crouch

and the severity of the promise of . . . . ment, the getting there, you didn't know a mountain had an . . . . how could you. She isn't really spending a thousand a week . . . . to the hospital to re up on bone saving hypnosis, it's a little more than that, or a little less, difficult to be exact unless you see the statements, tremendous to me still how the machine keeps perfect track. I wouldn't bother adding up. It'll only make you glue, something, right for holding a domed shoe together, three months that, maybe . . . . I don't understand how they don't keep records, or say no, but then again I never trained in the . . . . . of insistence. I used to think that limped was a word meaning very slow. It floors me too, seeing the rocks right down at the bottom, the water somehow even more clarified than air. When she gave me the fish I worried it would flee from something in the water, the water wrong, too clean or new or not new enough; an environment too lightly imbued with the fish itself, or not at all. It seemed sick when I cleaned the rocks and sick when I didn't, that's what kind of parent I would be, feeding the days to the treated water. I wrote to her today to say we love you, and travel safe, but I don't imagine she can receive even this without a minimum temperature of shame. But give it some time. I imagine poems will soon be written about all this in a language whose verb charts I once held out my hands for. You speak it though, and I want to say, you did everything you could. I want to tell you that, because it's true, and is it Spring that's doing it? Convoluting the metropolitan air with chirp, or is it because we've pulled all the doors in place. Almost daily I receive, as I know you do, the meetable and unmeetable lists of should. A long and seaming blade we know is searching through the wood.

Catching

Eva Birch

the sun is rising on the idea of being
centred in a lasso surrounding
all the paraphernalia that gives
light meaning

ropes woven into grasses
in the close-knit interior
faces waffled, signs of
that thing that leads to deep sleep

horses rubbing brow to flank
their reflections in the freshwater pool
unknown to the yabbies and
gallerist below

macramé-wrapped arms
brushing natural fibre mat
whipping custard to make a
vortex to the other side

my spiral hair from *Vertigo*
his ear from *Blue Velvet*
far-away lenses pointing to our
commons of enclosure

13

Love Object

Eva Birch

gingham comes from
genggang: ajar

stripes in primary colours
change each other square and open
designate what you could be
a man

ventilation casts stars
in the cotton while I sleep

black and red suit
folds into dual realms
home, hotel; kingdom, flagellation
bloody and renting

washing runs it
thinner in meaning

pinker now, a scarf
gestures décolletage
attachment style in fashion
for the people outside

tears find it
changing the feel but not the pattern

red and green doors
record the history of what you'll become
teddy bear, skirt
in my order of things

14

Homecoming Ceremony

Chen Yang

Don't move!
Don't move!

Even though I don't move
(my body temperature would reach 37.2°C or 37.3°C
if I moved)
they still shoot me from my neck to my wrist
(to see if I have fever or not).
That is why mom called
those who wear the protective coveralls,
protective goggles, and N95 respirators,
'violent philosophers'.
They always shoot you without hesitation,
then ask you —
Who are you?
Where are you from?
Where are you going?

—Xiamen International Airport, China (March 24)

Sydney Syndrome

Chen Yang

Symptoms: wear masks all the time, go to the
library ALONE, go to the gym ALONE, go
home ALONE, have lunch ALONE. Some patients will
experience delusions, such as believing
that the smell of bushfire is the smell of an unsuccessful
homemade hot-pot.

Susceptible individuals: Chinese international students.

Morbidity: almost 99.999%, especially in Spring Festival.

Risk of contagion: HIGH, and always defined as community-associated
infection.

PRESCRIPTION: GO HOME IMMEDIATELY ('go back to where you
came from').

16

Happy Chinese New Year, Sydney

Chen Yang

Reread *The Plague* by Camus
Chinese translation with
Chinese family and friends
digital mom, dad, grandpa, grandma
my phone screen full
onions should be cut into pieces
carrots and cabbages should be cleaned
'wear your mask, please'
grandma should say something to grandpa
smoky air resumes a couple
of days after rain smell
of burning hot-pot spreading
around the whole world

Survivor

Chen Yang

We allow the plastic to
obsess whales and bin chickens
the shape of struggling before death
= shape of
one-off coffee cup
one-off chopsticks
one-off meal packing boxes
one-off masks, gloves and protective coveralls
we allow ourselves to be survivors
in this way

today, I was a robber
in Broadway Shopping Centre, 8.30 a.m.
1kg jasmine rice = 1kg of hope
one small bag of toilet paper in Coles =
one small bag of thanks
I allow myself
to be a survivor in this way

18

Classifieds

Jackson C. Payne

His dad's war medals, framed on white card yellowed with moisture. The old television with the remote attached by an extension cord, once at a constant deafening volume but now cold and silent and dead. The never opened copy of his brother's book high on the bookshelf where no one can reach it. Pictures of the family the day they arrived by boat from England, him just a baby in his mother's arms, her staring past the camera, somehow looking like she's about to run; the rest of them all squinting into the Wellington wind, their hair helpless and twisted like trees. Staring at it Paul Patterson can hear the sound of the car behind them, can feel the violent drops of rain shooting from every direction but down. Of course he doesn't remember that day but sometimes he thinks he can.

The paper is spread out in front of him on the old coffee table, the one once covered with ashtrays piled high with twisted butts, half-forgotten cups of instant and weeks of the *Racing Express*. The detritus of a man who didn't care: his father. Although the coffee table is now polished clean, the ring stains of a thousand spills cover the surface like concussion stars. His father's elephantine impression on the couch sits open like a freshly dug grave. Paul sits next to it, walks past it, sometimes touches it, but never sits.

As a child, the Pattersons were visiting the grave of a family friend. Paul was skipping over the spongy winter grass when a wooden hand came across the top of his head. He stopped, his eyes stung as he squinted up at his dad's statue.

Don't you bloody walk on anyone's grave, boy. Have some respect.

Paul took that piece of advice, like all advice he'd received in his life, very seriously. He held it, smoothed it over, looked at it from all angles and then, when he was satisfied, filed it away to be dug out whenever necessary.

He studies the newspaper, running his finger down the personals until he finds what he's looking for. That curvy script and the not-so-subtle name that could be almost anyone doing the same thing anywhere in the world.

Still the same old phone, the kind where you pull the dial round with the finger hole and it dings an awful ding when it winds itself back. It rings and rings with no answer but finally he can hear the rasp of a woman who has smoked too many cigarettes; still feminine, but viscous.

Hey honey, you're speaking with Sugar.

Paul's nerves shoot through his body and he slams down the receiver. He looks around the room and thinks, Fuck, what would they say? His father's funeral brochure is resting on the mantel above where the fire used to be. In the picture on the brochure, Jack is leaning against a chicken wire fence, smiling. Paul doesn't remember that one. Nor does he remember ever seeing him smile like that, not in all the years it was just the two of them in that old house. His mother died when he was just a toddler and his brothers and sister left before he was a teenager so there was no chance of him doing the same. They weren't close, he and his father, but they orbited each other with the permanency of gravity, a scientific necessity for the working of all things.

The phone chimes with the sound of rusty bells and the reverberation on his legs makes him jump.

Hello.

Hey Paul, Kath. Listen, would you like to– waitaminute. Butch! Shush. It's just a fly.

Paul can hear the sound of china breaking and his sister's calls for the dog to stop, her bloated feet stomping through the tiny cottage she's turned into a hanging place for her lifelong knick-knacks and sentimentalities: wooden elephants from India and pictures of people she hasn't seen for three decades. It sounds like all her trinkets are tumbling to the ground. The phone crackles and scratches as Kath picks it back up.

Gonna have to call you back.

The dial tone whines in his ear before he can say goodbye. These phone calls have become somewhat commonplace with Kath. Her reaching out to talk about Christmas, no matter the time of year, wondering what to get everyone. She'd once suggested they go shopping on Boxing Day for presents for the following year. He always wondered how she'd coped alone all these years, having never seen her with anyone. At his dad's wake he'd walked in and caught the tail end of a conversation his brothers Jed and Will were having, sniggering into their club sandwiches.

…bloody lemon if you ask me.

Definitely a dyke–

They reddened when Paul sat down with them and asked plainly: *What's a dyke?*

On the mantel is a picture of his brothers, their arms chain-linked around each other, Will in a pink suit, Jed in a white one. They're both holding glasses with tiny paper umbrellas in them. In the distance are two women he's never seen before eyeing them eagerly.

Over the years his brothers rarely appeared at family events but when they came to the odd Christmas or birthday they did so with different women trailing behind them. Even their respective marriages seemed to be but passing flirtations, momentary excitedness followed by abrupt and inexplicable changes of heart. Not that Paul had ever talked to his brothers about that sort of thing, even if he knew what to say. How could he? To him there were no people cooler. Even the made-up pop stars on television paled in comparison. He didn't even mind that they had both been to jail; not that he would ever tell anyone.

He turns back to the paper in front of him, black words hammered into the page like thousands of tiny nails. Words scare him. He still hasn't replied to that letter Will sent for his birthday. He sat there for two hours with a dictionary open on his lap trying his best to make sense of it. He only got the bit about the film script Will had written, some famous actress from *Shortland Street* playing the main part. She had the hots for him, he said.

There's a knock at the door. Paul checks his watch and knows exactly who it is. The faded red carpet stretches toward the front door like dried blood. Through the frosted glass Paul can see her purple-grey perm and feature window glasses, the same as she's always been.

Mrs Anderson, hullo! he says, opening the door.

Young Paul.

She has always called him Young Paul, even though he is now deep in his forties. He leans down to kiss her, his large back like a motorway on-ramp. Paul is tall but next to Mrs Anderson he looks like something from a fairy tale.

She visits at six-thirty every Wednesday with a basket of scones and has done as long as he can remember. She started just after his mother died. He long ago stopped eating scones but his colleagues at the tobacco factory love Thursday mornings because they know they can have a fresh one at smoko. He doesn't tell her this but suspects she knows: how could one man eat twelve cheese scones in a week?

You well?

Aye, Paul. So long as these legs can carry me.

She moves down the corridor ahead of him and into the living room.

What you looking to buy? she says, pointing to the newspaper lying open with outstretched arms.

A painful knot of shame pulls tight in his stomach.

Oh, ah, an um… a bed.

Mrs Anderson's eyes fall upon Paul, her intense prescription glasses magnifying her scrupulousness. She seems to find what she's looking for in his face and turns away, puts the scones on the kitchen table near the portrait of his mother, the one taken just after she won a South London beauty contest before the war. In it, his mother's eyes look forward but not past the camera, like she is in all other photos he has of her. For that, he loves this picture most. His mother is a scrapbook of other people's memories, tidbits and quotes stuck together with homemade paste watered down too much; every time he turns the page something becomes unstuck and falls away. The portrait has come to feel like the only thing that has remained undiluted.

It has occupied many places in the kitchen and lounge room but, no matter where it's moved, Mrs Anderson finds it and puts the scones in front of it, like some sort of religious offering. Paul has never thought to ask why she does this but, from time to time, enjoys putting the picture in places Mrs Anderson must squint to find.

I best be going, love. Housie starts on the hour.

She never stays long and for this he is glad. The certainty of her visits is the last of an old routine borne out of his mother's death. She stops and looks at the newspaper momentarily, looks back up at Paul, and continues to the front door.

Bye Mrs Anderson.

Goodbye.

On the landing she turns to him once more, a sadness ageing her face further than its eighty-four years.

You know, there's a spare room at ours. If you want.

Thanks, Mrs Anderson. But I've not lived anywhere else.

If you change your mind…

The loose panes of glass rattle as he closes the front door. Through it, the faint outline of her perm disappears into the late evening blue as she waddles stiffly down the garden path.

As a teenager, his brother Jed had stood at that same door in tears, saying goodbye and hugging his mum, everyone else frightened at the sudden departure of the one who, when no one else would own up, had quietly taken all those beatings from their father. During the goodbyes he just sat on the couch with the television on. When Jed called out, his father turned up the volume.

Back on the couch Paul again traces the column until he reaches the number. He calls it but this time a voice leaps out instantly.

We've got caller ID you fuckin' pervert. Stop calling here, alright?

Ah, I ah, um…

I said fuck off!

The clack of her phone slamming somehow hurts his ear. He wonders how that is possible. He moves his finger down the column a little further and finds another advertisement he hadn't previously seen. Closing his eyes, Paul takes several deep breaths and then brings the rotary dial of the phone around. The tone sounds for just half a ring when an even deeper rasp comes from the receiver; Paul thinks smoking cigarettes must come hand in hand with this line of work.

Queen Candy. What's your pleasure?

Oh hello. I'm, uh, wondering if you have any appointments available. Tonight?

Sure thing darling. How's eight-thirty?

Fine.

After Paul hangs up he tries watching television but can't concentrate. He checks his watch: there is still an hour and a half. He takes his coat from the hook by the door and puts on his father's old cheese cutter hat, the one worn away at the peak. The frost is already settling on the grass and the chill of it makes him shiver as he pulls the garden gate closed. Above him, the velvet night is speckled with sequined stars. He pauses at the roundabout on the corner: to the right is the orange glow of town where he goes each day to work; to the left is the Coast Road, unpaved, unlit, and stretching all the way to the sea. He steps off the edge of the road, the metal crunching beneath his feet as he moves into the dark.

19

Brilliant Underpinnings
of Future Regret

Magdalena Kozlowski

Take it! Your invitation
to revel with us in the back garden.
When you get tired, or inspired, from
hills-hoist bags of

Sweet

Fruity

White

there's always room on the couch, but
the brush
turkey has his mound, and his rounds

to make before bedtime.

Wicked window to bedroom eyes, blinking
as the doily curtains grate
against the windshield,

and you hope the van's disguised.

Sunset chills your goosebumps
through soggy towel.

Dope-fiend fascinations, worn-out Wettex,
laminated couches hugging
                              sawn-off arse cheeks,
slack
from watching Joss Whedon's *Serenity* (2005).

Corrugated corduroy
cushions serrate

sweat-silted forehead, some time after
the radio goes off.

Fibres to be exhumed from the flypaper
of your throat,
and flavour just as bad.

Something of the vaporous chlorine
coaxed by the sun's morning fingertips
invading the patio,

the laughter left in you
is weighty – and prodding your eyes to

wake up
like the concrete
                    you can smell.

20

Pulling Up the Walls[1]

Joan Fleming

Contact is crisis.[2] In 2020, people in cities all over the world learned how not to touch one another. But touch – whether physical or moral, emotional or imaginary – has always been a challenge to the idea of the fixed boundaries of the self.

In my life, I have lived in Melbourne, Madrid, Wellington, Denver, Toronto, and Dunedin. Life in these cities is engineered to keep us apart from one another. You may not feel this on the bus or the subway, but we have houses and apartments. We have wardrobes and faucets. We have walls.

In camp life, in Aboriginal Australia, I have felt the boundaries of the self start to shimmer and give. Contact has stung, irritated, and confounded. It has made me sick. It has also made me smaller, and larger. Made me see myself as a part, not a whole.

As a whitefella (*Kardiya*) spending time in the desert, I used to worry a lot about how to achieve the position of someone touchable. How could I overcome the (warranted) distrust of those who continually receive the message that they, themselves, are untouchable: physically, psychically, emotionally, culturally? Come to school, say the Kardiya, but we won't teach 'language' (*Warlpiri*). Come and buy petrol at the roadhouse, but stay out of

---

1   Note: This essay has been read for cultural sensitivity by Ned Vaughan Hargraves at Pintubi Anmatjere Walrpiri Media (PAW Media) and approved for publication. Of the essay, Ned said: 'It was to the point. It was hard. Sad and hard. But she had to tell it. It is good to tell that from Kardiya point of view. I felt things, many things.'

2   'Dirt and Desire: The Phenomenology of Female Pollution in Antiquity,' in *Men in the Off Hours* by Anne Carson, Cape Poetry, 2000.

the restaurant. What does it mean to become someone touchable? For me, it has meant sharing to the point of risk. Giving away the last of the petrol money. Using the spoon after it's been cleaned by licking.

The last winter I was up in the desert, in 2018, we were carting round a grandmother's painting-in-progress in the back of the Toyota. The paint went everywhere. My borrowed swag and my travel backpack got clouded blue. I didn't mind. I also didn't mind anymore saying *no* sometimes to the Warlpiri family I travel with – a word that, five years ago, I struggled to get out of my mouth. My time up in the desert consists of a strange oscillation between making myself touchable, and withdrawing from the risks of touch. Holding boundaries, letting them slip. I miss the desert. I don't think I can live there.

Touch

Nangali must have been six or seven in 2016. Maybe five. 'She's mad one,' the family say – with affection – because of her sweet private fairy-tale sing-songing at the world. She has huge wet eyes that send light back, and framed in the window of a donga at the nature reserve where her mob do Indigenous Ranger work, or on her back in the middle of the sweeps of a snow-angel she's made in the red dirt, she is as photogenic as a cliché National Geographic cover child. The family go off for their day of Ranger work and Nangali and I stay back at camp, both scribbling in our way. As a child, I was fey like that. In the afternoon, I insist she have a shower and, lacking flannels, I get the crud off her behind with my hands. A clean shirt is a relatively clean *something* from the family pile inside the donga. We'll do a wash tomorrow. There are washing machines in the shed, next to the box freezer whose lid is difficult to close on its overflow of frozen feral cats. It took me a while to work out who Nangali's 'real' mum was. She must be in her late 20s, but she has a restless, trapped-in teenager vibe. Dark tattoo lines radiate from the edges of her eyes like makeup. She's smart, sharp. Now she's living down near Adelaide somewhere.

In 2018, Nangali is a little taller, and not much less fey. We are staying at the nature reserve again. Her grandma and auntie do a food run back to the community – we have root vegetables and long-life milk, but no bread, no fresh meat – leaving me and F., a friend from Melbourne, to distract Nangali from her lonely-crying. I show her photos on my phone of Kuala Lumpur,

Portugal, Madrid. 'Magic,' she whispers, squeaky-breathless, at a photo of a temple mural, a seven-headed statue of Krishna. 'Magic' is a medieval relic, 'magic' is a Lisbon street art stencil of an anatomical heart. Grandma and auntie come back well after dark and growl her for crying. 'Why you lonely!' they say. 'They're kin for you! That's family!' They've built some new shower blocks for the reserve's volunteers, and walking on the fresh-mopped lino feels unearned after only three days in the bush. Even the sawdust for the composting toilets is weirdly scented. I am singing out, 'Shower time! Shower time, Nangali!' I am trying not to feel like my missionary grandmother who bathed the children at Yuendumu every Sunday before church in the big copper. In a lot of books, I have seen the same photograph of her, young, in a starched white dress, bathing the children who have lined up so nicely. That white dress would have been smeared red mere minutes after they put away the cameras. I share most things with this mob but I usually refuse to share my towel. I am often feeling like my grandmother and often trying not to feel like my grandmother.

Risks

F. manages to keep whatever it is at bay until we hit the Alice Springs town limits, and she becomes suddenly exhausted and asks me to take the wheel. We had planned to cook an enormous veggie stir fry and go out drinking and complain about town life with its billboards and its car dealerships and mourn that the trip was over – only ten days! what possessed us to think that would be 'enough' time? – but she goes straight to bed and doesn't leave until the diarrhoea starts around midnight. I take her temperature every few hours, try to make her drink tea. It's not the gastro symptoms that worry me, it's the shivering, the full body aches, the collapsing in the bathroom. It was her first time going bush with me, though we'd talked about it for years. The next day she seems a little better, and then much, much worse. In the clinic waiting room she can't sit on the chair for the pain in her stomach. I won't forget how she writhed on the doctor's examining table, her feet in borrowed crocs making a sad triangle as she pumped her legs and the doctor depressed her stomach, feeling for I don't know what. She couldn't stifle her cries. Contact is crisis.

A mate of my uncle's who lives near the hospital drops off a bag of fast food. A godsend. I growl a plucky Yapa (*Central Desert Aboriginal*) woman who tries to nick it off the window ledge outside the triage of the emergency ward, where I leave it while I help my friend inside. I had not eaten McDonalds in something like eight years. Desperate measures. 'I'm hungry!' she mimes through the thick glass. 'Leave it!' I mime back. 'I'm hungry too!' When we finally get her into emergency, things move swiftly. Morphine, an IV. Fluid drip after drip. Blood tests every six hours. Endless days in a windowless isolation ward, plugging and unplugging the drip machine every half an hour to drag it squeaking to the bathroom. My friend has something the doctors diagnose as shigella. It is a dysentery bug, a nasty one, and highly infectious. In the end, she shat blood for four days because she touched something – a piece of food – that had *matter* on it, that had the virus on it. *In* it. Almost three months later, she's finally feeling normal again.

I have been sick too. One year at a sports' weekend in a neighbouring community, a fastidious after-hours nurse paged through her dog-eared manual and told me it would be best if I went back to town for some tests because there was a risk I had *heart fever*, although the internet tells me that heart fever is not a thing. Did she think I had rheumatic fever? Maybe I had the flu. Maybe it was culture shock.

When the boundaries of the built self get soft, there is a letting in, and sometimes it shows itself as sickness. Every time I get back to Alice Springs after a trip, I buy a tube of scabies cream and a lice comb. I no longer need the viscous white stuff they call 'barrier cream' to stop out the sun and wind. Instead, I start wearing the cosmetic armours of my gender: *mascara*, from the nineteenth-century Italian for *mask*. I wash my clothes, hang them out to dry. Wet things dry fast in the desert. I crave the exquisite, risky porousness that camp life and the bush can give, then I get back to town and I smear back on my boundaries, comb out the creatures that communal life lets nest there. This is a conflict I never feel easy with. I am a whitefella. I can move between these worlds as I like. And though the walls feel bad at first, I pull them back up around me, because I can.

Cleanliness

My missionary grandmother Pat's diaries detail a life of porous intercultural penetration. She and my grandfather went 'to live among the natives' and teach them to worship. Over twenty-five years she cultivated huge affection, but hated every grain of dirt. Her diaries relate her efforts to keep home and hearth in proper order. Civilized. Acceptable. *Clean.* To keep the walls pulled up. And yet, every day and everywhere were the hazards of touch.

How did my grandmother touch, and what did she do with her recoiling? I could say that Pat privately castigates the Yapa for their smells and their habits, and I privately castigate myself. I could say that living with the dirt is an initiation for me, and for her it was a battle. I could say that she wished to teach, and I wish to be taught. All of this is true, and none of it is sufficient.

In her diary for the year 1950, Tom and Pat's first year at Yuendumu, the word 'clean' appears 34 times. Ten years later, in 1960, the word 'clean' appears zero times. Did she acclimatise? Did the rigidity of her boundaries soften somewhat? The entries for the year 1950 narrate a literal pulling-up of walls, as she and my grandfather Tom toiled to make the tin shack they landed in liveable, and to come around to the isolation and the weathering and the thousand subtle Warlpiri refusals and the red dust. Entry after entry is about cleaning the sheets, the clothes, the house, the dog, my father's gluey eye, the 'natives.' But looking at the 1960 diary, the text is spare. She was busy. She records in extreme brevity a flood of people coming and going over her threshold, a constant visitation of bodies and personalities and community dramas in which she was intimately implicated. The preoccupation with cleanliness does not disappear. After visiting friends in town, she writes, 'Nice house they have here, needs me to keep it shining.' However – and this is a relief for me to say – the names and cares of the people who bound her to the desert take narrative and psychic precedence over the habits of the dust and grease. People, it seems, began to matter more than cleanliness.

Brutalities

I am cross-legged at the edge of Nyirrpi, enjoying a sliver of cat meat. Cat meat, fresh from the earth oven, and some incongruous avocado and tuna on rice cracker which the kids crowd round to say 'manda' for (*gimme*). After tasting it, they make a 'yuck' face. Some animal welfare types a few years ago got stirred up after reading that the Indigenous Rangers kill the cats with a crowbar. I suppose it sounds cruel? The word itself – *crowbar. Trap* sounds more scientific, I suppose. More Western. But it is precision crowbar work these women do. It is very swift. There is a target, they hit it. A single blow to the head.

A restaurateur at a roadhouse between Alice Springs and Yuendumu once told me his off-season side-hustle was culling camels (another pest) from helicopters. They cull them with machine guns. I imagined a yahoo slaughter: panicked herds of sweetly eyelashed camels sprayed with bullets and collapsing into mangled piles. In reality, the helicopter circles the herd and they cluster together, bothered by the curious noise. Then they string out into their natural line, and start walking again. The helicopter, flying low, picks them off one by one with a bullet to the back of the head.

I have needed to flick my desert preconceptions out the window like ash – my romanticisations and my nightmare images both. The brutalities of the desert are less *Apocalypse Now*, more *Brazil*. It's the bureaucratic obfuscations, where Yapa needs meet whitefella systems, that are so hard to swallow. That, and the treatable diseases, the high suicide rates, the deaths in custody, the familial traumas that get handed on, that 'deepen like a coastal shelf.'[3]

The cat is good. It tastes like chicken. The day is cool and bright. All contradiction is in cohabitation here. This is a hard and good life, in a place that early maps of Australia marked 'useless.' What grows here? Mulberry, bush coconut, spinifex, she-oaks, and all things human.

No

I get a phone call every few months asking me for a credit card transfer to help with a grocery shop. Usually I can afford it. When the requests ramp up around Christmas time, with phone calls coming every week, I start saying no. When I visit, too, it's give and take. Everyone pitches in for food, fuel, meat, and, sure, tobacco, though I know it's a curse.

We've talked about splitting the royalties for the forthcoming poetry book, but these are poetry royalties, I say, not mining ones. There's a bit of a difference in scale. If something I write about the desert wins a prize, we agree, we'll split the winnings. If it's a big prize, it could buy them a Toyota.

The dance of request and pushback is what family do among themselves, all the time. But requests from the family towards us, the whitefellas, seem to ramp up towards the end of a trip. The women in particular are master hunter-gatherers. They hunt and gather lizards, witchetty grubs, bush

---

3   Phillip Larkin, 'This be the verse,' from *Phillip Larkin Poems: Selected by Martin Amis*, Faber & Faber, 2012.

tomatoes, kangaroo, bush turkeys. They also hunt-and-gather warm clothes, car tools, billies, cooking wires, and money. The men, though, have the strangest requests: 'Nungarrayi (*my skin name*), you gotta send a gold watch. And one of those big blankets, the ones you wear.' *A poncho?* 'Yeah, and that big hat too.' *You want a poncho and a sombrero?* 'Yeah, then I'll be sitting in my own shade!'

I'm not going to send a gold watch, given my poet-teacher's salary, and this mob's loose relationship with the notion of time. I'll send a warm jumper, long skirts for the women, sometimes tobacco, photos, and a $50 note in a card, telling my news. Being able to send money, what I can, from Melbourne, is a way of keeping in touch – something I don't want to lose.

Home

I am in my uncle's house in Alice Springs, cradling the trembling heap of a little brown camp dog who is experiencing his first-ever trip to town as terror, confusion, and crisis. I am virus-sick with the unnamed thing after the sports' weekend, and I have driven back to town with this little dog in tow, at the family's insistence, because little dogs are popular and get 'lost' (taken) and this one belongs to an anthropologist friend who is on holiday, and besides, 'You need company, Nungarrayi.' His name is Brownie. Because he is brown.

Some camp dogs have names, and some don't. In some Indigenous communities, the dogs with names are kin in a way that designates them as children; in other communities, the kin names designate them as parents. Some belong to people and families and are beloved and fed and taken on trips, and some creep and rally round the boundaries of the communities of Nyirrpi and Yuendumu, nameless and belonging to no-one. But they all seem to run together. It is common to see camp dogs attempting to eat the least probable 'food' items, like the feathers of a freshly plucked turkey. Once, on Territory weekend, I saw a dog running with a lit firecracker in its mouth. There might be a broader dog pecking order on the communities' fringes, with secret periphery dog bosses. But within the world of the camp, the hierarchy is ordered by human affection, and at the top of the hierarchy are the little dogs. In a Toyota crammed with mountains of blankets and bulky paintings and human bodies and their belongings, little dogs can squeeze in without burden. They also keep you warm at night. Though

I sometimes failed to shove off the family dogs who amassed on top of my swag of an evening, Brownie is the only dog I ever let transgress the boundary from *outside* to *inside*. That trip, he started sleeping inside my swag with me. Other whitefellas, like the Ranger Coordinators, found this level of intimacy distasteful, but I was grateful for it. So was Brownie. He could move from lap to camp periphery and back with total freedom and total protection. Lucky dog.

Now, however, we are sleeping inside a whitefella house, and the rules are bewildering. My uncle's glossy, stocky, overfed yellow-lab cross, named Missy, is frighteningly territorial. My uncle is worried for Brownie. A few years ago, a fight over a bone in the back garden resulted in Missy giving my uncle's older dog what can most accurately be described as a 'braining.' I say to my uncle, Brownie is a camp dog. He can handle himself. But we are not out in open country here. We are inside, and this is Missy's world. The dogs are suspiciously acquainting themselves with each other in the living room, when Brownie does a strange thing. With his teeth, he takes hold of the corner of a white doily that has fallen to the floor – a doily surely belonging to my late Grandmother – and, with great delicacy, he pulls it over the top of Missy's half-full food bowl. It is odd boundary work, a type of burying. Missy pounces – it happens suddenly – and Brownie gives off a high-pitched alarm squeal. I find I am growling in my lowest, loudest voice, the voice the women have taught me to use to scare off the cheeky dogs. I scoop Brownie up and carry him from the room.

For the next few days of my convalescence, I coddle Brownie in a cloistered world of walls and shut doors and I watch him become fretful and shivery and refuse his food. After he runs across a busy intersection, I start keeping him on a leash. I give him his first-ever bath. It's a bind: here I am, bathing a camp dog called 'Brownie' and freighting him with whitefella-world anxieties in order to keep him from being brained. To keep him safe from risks, I have made him into a creature at odds with himself.

Waste

It's Territory Weekend, the only weekend of the year when fireworks are sold in the shop. We're camped at Emu Bore, waiting for the rest of the family to hurry up and get back from whatever tasks of knotted family negotiations have delayed them in Nyirrpi. We want to set off the fireworks.

F. and I and the grandmother make dinner on the fire, dispensing totally with the polite formulations that order the rituals of dinner in my own culture: 'Could you please pass me the butter?' and 'Would anyone like to split the last sausage?' Those politenesses don't work out here. The tools and fixings of dinner are strewn all round the fire and everyone's in reach of something essential. So it's *'Manda* butter' or *'Manda* that knife.' The gimmes used to strike my ears, they used to feel rude, gruff. Now, I see, it's just easy. I used to haul my body right up off the ground when I needed something on the other side of the fire. I used to drink in the smoke, cough it back out again. Now I just say *manda*.

After dinner, they still haven't returned, and we don't want to wait. The night is still. The quiet water tower and the granddaddy ghost gum, nothing but murmuring land for miles. So we light a fuse and send up the dangerous light that shouts as it touches the sky. Nangali's eyes are silver with fear and pleasure. We are whooping, our faces upturned.

For some reason, though, I insist we ration ourselves. It's a box of twenty, but 'just two' I say. 'We should save the rest.' Why? What perfect time was I insisting we wait for? The others return too late, we are already asleep, and the next day they leave on a Ranger trip, and there is a scramble about where to stash the remaining fireworks.

F. and I take a couple with us on our drive back to town. We find a camp spot off the dirt highway on the road between Papunya and Ormiston, a place with a soft feeling in the dusk, a *held* sort of feeling. It's our last night in the beautiful open. But when we set off a firework, it feels wrong. The dark is too dark. We don't have the family with us, for protection and company. The festivity feels misplaced. Visions of danger and threat implanted by images from slasher films fill our imaginations, and we do not want to announce ourselves.

That other night at Emu Bore, we ought to have wasted the fireworks. We ought to have set off six, a dozen, the whole bang lot. Without restrictions, and without counting, we might have indulged our thirst for the moment, and let the sky be filled with colour. At this moment, on our way back to town, halfway between worlds, we want to be unseen, unfound, untouched. In fact, we wish we had walls right now.

21

A Tableaux Vivant for Jenny

Savanna Wegman

Jenny has decided
wild stallions, swans,
ducklings and shy pink metallic cobras
belong in a garden
of tiny houses
that frame our front porches

sculpt small hands for Jenny
and try forgetting rules

(For example: not real reality, true imagined real,
not real true, lies and escape fantasy, the fact that cobras
aren't safe and can kill people and horses too especially
if they're untrained and neither can be brought into
suburbia to live in a garden with very small homes and
we would need a larger fence and stock up on food and
warn the neighbours)

She says *everything is saturated and glowing and lush*
and blooming like parachutes nothing is still
everything unfolds
She says she knows *the meaning of mystery goosebumps*
and fake dress ups and princess parties and nice weather
and rose bushes and
science in the sky –

She is building swans from beautiful things and
we will just have to watch

22

Stage Dances

Savanna Wegman

1.   *[They dance a waltz with spiders in their pockets
and freckles on their cheeks. They step on each
other with cold tip toes wearing masks of forest
animals. The lips of their masks kiss.]*

2.   *[A solo cowgirl swings her hat on her index
finger masked in black, she moves her hips and her
shoulders in a repeated rhythm slow, sultry and
hypnotic. She is surrounded by mirrors. Spotlights move
through her and she is translucent.]*

3.   *[All characters on stage burst. The air is blazing.
There is silence.]*

4.   *[The GODS descend as black and white acrobats
from the sky to the sounds of dark jazz.]*

5.   *[Thunder and lightning and blood and fighting
and rain and darkness and gore and violence and swords
and guns and flame tipped arrows and knives and poison
and unnatural death and rotten food and pain and
sadness and laughter and victory.]*

6.   *[The stage is still and then it breathes.]*

7.   *[The CREATURES onstage are made of velvet and raw meat. They perform a melancholy ballet for The KING. It's beautifully haunting.]*

8.   *[A group of young girls appear from the light dressed like the pope.]*

9.   *[A dead army of cloaked soldiers kneel together and silently cry. The stained curtain slowly falls, covering them from above.]*

10.   *[The CHORUS whisper softly to each other. One member falls and another one rises.]*

23

Girls on Film

Savanna Wegman

We match Kodachrome prints to recreate historic sweethearts
/ underground riots powering a freak noise / war cries sooth
trauma like healing oil / angry laugher excavates a lust to
detonate / glossy skin mixes shared sweat and collective fury
avoids beauty / being beautiful / beautifulness / essential are
weaponised utensils like sickly sweet lip balm flavoured
strawberry pop / skinny dripping hair exposed to moonlight /
equip to defend and text me when you get home / homemade
espresso martinis in coffee mugs elongate night time
 conversations / one day to glow in magnificent nostalgia /
attract sisterhood, self-care and Suzy's kind of unapologetic
confidence / bubble bathing with soggy books / textured tips
/ always kiss with your eyes wide open / quick text never
baby / disguise in spiked guava juice / gummy vitamins
/ smile through spaghetti / find five minutes to cry / sneak
television and re-enact queens of noise with the Omnichord /
lingerie themed tomato soup tea party / a ritual for skin
purification and increased sexual aura / ferocious
performance / stockings stretched making faceless / static
conversation channels into new voice box / predators DIY
bedazzle with glomesh singlets / crunchy hankies on public
transport / amplify the infernal karaoke sung upon the
sweetest of sixteens

24

Walking Home

Riya Rajesh

'Ma'am!' the shop vendor shouts in your direction as you walk away, distracted by the flashing lights ahead. He shoves the sarees back into their plastic pockets with the tired frustration of another sale lost. The scent of sandalwood incense lightens with every step you take. You look back at the man, surrounded by linen and sequins, wondering if he'll break even tonight. You turn away.

He mumbles in Tamil and you catch a word here and there, struggling for the translation. It has been so long since you've been here. So long since you spoke your language. Melbourne's intonations have been pressed into your mouth. Eventually, your mind allows the words to drift into Chennai's heavy air. They dissipate there, accepted by the heat.

Saravana Stores sits on the busy street, its flashing neon sign towering over the smaller shops. Inside is a mad scramble. A family is huddled over a microwave. A woman is admiring a watch. Another is brushing hands with her partner, as they stand in line for the change rooms. Two people, strangers to each other, reach for the same kettle; they touch, blush, and apologise. Eventually, everyone will gather at the payment counters, where tired workers are bagging items. This is the machinations of a Friday night. At the cashier, the family will feel embarrassed by the spread of purchases on the countertop: handbags, shoes, and colourful toy cars – microwave forgotten. They will look in sympathy, or perhaps shame, at the cashier's hands. But then they will walk out and forget. You know this movement. Muscle memory, behind the chaos. It holds a strange universality – a relative comfort. *This is home*, you tell yourself.

You blink and shake the imprint of the store sign from your eyes, as you turn away. Behind you, a man is walking out with three bags in each hand. The plastic is bulging and stretching. He lives in the very corner of your eye, as versions of him always have. Early moonlight glints off his too-new leather shoes. His face draws in the shadows of the darkening sky and your bones feel suddenly hollow. You don't need uncomfortable closeness to know his pupils are dilated behind heavy eyelids. Unblinking. His stillness is so grotesquely familiar, it compels your quick footsteps forward. 'Look at her… those tight pants,' his voice in your head says, his eyes staring at the skin between your waistband and your shirt. 'Slut.' You realise there is no difference between a man leering here and a man leering there. His gaze anywhere makes your skin shed. You hasten your footsteps. *This is home.*

A mannequin is hanging from a lamppost ahead, clad in a pomegranate-red churidar. You can almost see a blue necklace rattling against her throat, bangles clinking at her wrists, her hand clasped in another's. She shifts in the wind and looks down at you, expressionless. She sees your fear, you hope.

The city talks over your thoughts. Swerving motorbikes hinder your panicked steps. It's getting late. The thought of tomorrow's early morning flight pinches the nerves around your eyes. You've forgotten the fear almost instantly, or maybe forgotten is the wrong word. The fear has recessed into the middle-ground of your mind, ready to be reactivated another time. Soon, you will fly over this city, watching from an air-conditioned distance. You'll return though, in a few years, maybe more. It's the migrant-duty, isn't it?

The sun has almost set. Uniformed children flick their plaited hair as they run past you, scrambling towards the moving bus. They need to be home for sambar and rice. They need to lie to their parents about after-school tuition. One slips, skids across yesterday's rain. Falls. There is a fierceness in her eyes that you will never have. Not with your poor-little-rich-girl factory-ripped jeans. The girl gets up. She glances at you for a second and can't help but see an intruder. She sees whitewashing, you're sure. But you're blocked from further imagining as she disappears into the bus, her ribbon left behind in the caking mud.

Clambering on behind her is a young woman. Her pale thighs are stark against Chennai's warm dusk; an inverse shadow. The beads on her hands jangle as she readjusts her backpack. *Gucci* is embroidered on the straps. You're reminded of the *Gvccii* bags a few stalls away, with a wry smile. She's a tourist, you assume, and distaste sours your mouth. Layers of sweat keep her bhindi from sticking to her forehead. It flails and falls, settling into the gravel by the bus's tyres. She's trying her best to find poverty endearing. Probably here to 'balance her chakras' or take sympathetic selfies with the 'poor locals'. When she returns home, her social media will flood with culture. You cringe at her love for a city that both is and isn't yours.

But you are suddenly surprised. She asks the driver something in mangled Tamil, shouting over the engine's rumble, unable to mould her mouth into the 'rh' sound. He answers her. And yet, you can't decipher their words. Maybe, 'When does this bus leave?' Or, 'How long will it take?' You keep walking.

This is home, you tell yourself. *I am deaf here and this is home.*

You slow your steps when the scent of sandalwood returns, drifting from the incense sticks. Time has reduced them to crumbling stumps, sticking upright out of a green banana. You've arrived at the same saree shop. It is discoloured in this new darkness, weighed down by the sticky air. You wonder if the owner will recognise you. By the entrance, a woman is rubbing red fabric between her fingers. Her son is tugging at the sequins on a saffron-coloured blouse, while the vendor speaks quietly. He knows it is too late for desperation and his customer is already distracted. You look away.

You're here for something, aren't you? Here for a reason. Your flight leaves tomorrow. You'll be soaring. And when you take off, Chennai will not wait for your return.

25

Tassels and Degrees

Soumik Deb

Hustle and bustle means nothing, you see.
Fold the wooden membrane, my
mind, and call me sister—call me,
sister. Filth, caps and degrees starch
my life, lift me higher. Burn

my inner shell into spun, stringy obsidian
and blow my glass frame into a tyre. Roll me
down the steps and reward me with paper praise.
Sit between my thistle frames and tell me you tolerate me.
I am obsessed with the way you sniff the putrid air around my work,
concrete pigeon. You mean nothing

in the grand scheme of tuition, the fruits of my
excessive breath. I sweat a big game,
I lie to my ego's reflection and tell him
'I love that your hair is shit and your mouth tilts
when I tell you I love that I can finish when I want to
without complaining; I'm sore and I can't be bothered'.

You see, I need you,
I loved you and put you above this fleshy
lemon-meringue existence. If you are a skyscraper,
I want no part of your adolescent
super-structure. I need the end, yours

and mine. I am selfish. I am understood completely
in all my gall and guts,
my glory and gristle. Spartacus rules my mind,
Magni grips my feet growling
Edda at my success. Succumb to the hoarfrost, keel
forward and mark my passage.

Tell me I am a name to look at,
I have become one of you after all.

Am I Gallipoli or Rwanda?
Some mental trench in the gap of packed libraries?
In turn we jump, one by one, crying
over Bundy rum, failed papers.
Puppet on plastic links,
make me dance.

26

Faith

Stacy Chan

Do you speak to your god about me?

When we are in fatigue's protection, when the rain has
boxed us into gifts for the greater world,

Then, when you are huddled in your chains and your
faith, do you speak to your god about me? If I had a god

I would feel as indignant as oblivion
but I have been taught otherwise and see here:
this is a body you have created,
they had to cut it out of you like cancer.

But do you speak to your god about me?
Or has his silence compelled you to slaughter me?
You would kill me if your god told you to.
You would kill yourself if your god told you to.
Me, whose fingers you pulled like wheat noodles just so
you could suck on the tendons.
Me, who wore your slippery skin when the hunters had
found your workplace.
Me, whose back bends like a question mark around the
first explosion.

I will not drown in the icy ravine just to fish your lonely
coins.
Your god will not be there when you pull the trigger,
he will be a golden necklace around your neck catching
the wink of the dying star,
and his son who is not your son,
will not accompany you in the driveway wondering why
we have not yet

Returned home.

27

Identity Politics

Stacy Chan

I am a body split by light,

my shadow pretends to be me in the morning;

one of me seeks the broad shoulders of the cross
while the shadow converses with the pastor about
candles and women; they are both the same you know,
waxy and hot and easily drowned

and both reside in my bedroom;

I whisper to her – my flesh whispers, that is, to
the shadow – that they can't see me with the lights out so
don't be afraid to kiss me there and there and certainly
there

for tomorrow when the sun creates me, I will
have to mount the decomposing form of the heterosexual
divine, moan *yes* marriage is certainly interesting and *yes*
the parliament was disgraceful in allowing this to happen
and *yes* dicks are great *yes* I only live to get some;

and my parents have been waiting years for me to
kidnap one but I don't know how to break it to them that
they have yet to go extinct – "I'll lend you my net so you

can join the Facebook group where they were doing raids
by the train station" – meanwhile I have her between my
legs in prayer and I'm sure God would understand

     that they've tried to fuse me so many times at
golden hour, when I'm stretched content and faceless
across the front porch, I feel angry enough to pounce,
instead,

     I become the light that splits the house,

     there is a chasm between the living room and the
kitchen which creates an unbearable draft in winter, and I
have to chronically lie by telling the truth until things
make sense, like:

     (I am a simile split by *as*)

     I am as straight as a wishbone and equally
unbreakable

     I am as happy as the colour red

     I am as invisible as death

28

Love Poem

Stacy Chan

You remind me of someone, standing too close
in a crowded elevator where no one is talking.
Maybe I had met you before, long ago in a
                    biological way
when the first fish crawled on land
& suffocated on the thought of one day becoming
the fire and the crumbling ash, or when looking up
with its dark pupils it saw death in a feather boa
                    circling. At least
you haven't evolved into some disfigured animal
stalking suburban fence lines—
instead I've conceded the privacy of my anatomy
to your tools warmed by the touch of other bodies. But
for God's sake commit to my human mortality
                    & not those sly
ideas of a hungry darkness which drink
consciousness like boxed wine, making me believe that
you would rather pass out in a strange room, corroding
from the inside, than submit to the past.

29

A Way In

Parth Sharma

In Mernda, where I live, I keep finding abandoned houses. At last count there were seven, at varying distances from my own residence. I would go searching around the semi-rural neighbourhood, along road skirts and down side streets, and nestled in the tall, dead grass would be a structure. The roof would invariably have holes, and the exterior paint would be peeling away as if chipped at by bored, invisible children. The window-panes would be empty, with glass lying around beneath, spread out, shattered and jagged.

For a 'developing' suburb, Mernda has a long history. Migrants have settled in this locale for almost 150 years. There is an ancient post office which dates back to 1875. The Bridge Inn Hotel, built in 1891, is still around, still has its original red brick façade, and is still consistently visited, though no one spends the night anymore. There are a few churches from the same period dotted around the area, most made of dark, weathered stone. It is an old town, built on the land of the Wurundjeri people. The nature of 'home', then, has meant many different things to the many people who have lived here.

*

When I enter an abandoned house, I cannot help but wonder who lived there before. Home has often been metaphorised as a womb: a place where we are kept alive, grow up and are formed. For most of history, the house you were born in, you stayed in and passed on to your children, like the genetic story of our bodies. But the connection of home to body is multifaceted. What happens to one can happen to the other. Houses grow old, as we do. They usually outlast us. And just like we leave the womb, occasionally we leave houses.

Sometimes the leaving is sudden, and what is left behind is not destroyed, necessarily, but is surrendered to time like a stone thrown into a river. An abandoned house appears to be static, in that time flows around and above it, but this illusion belies the fact that a slow, slow wearing down has begun. Microcurrents of moments pass, sloughing off bits of the whole. Windows shatter, doors unhinge and sigh to the floor, the floorboards warp into mountains. The paint-chips outside curl like rubber bands – taut to breaking point – and then ping! they fall off, joining the million other bits below.

Eventually, the home becomes porous. After all, when people move out, everything else moves in: branches grow through busted windows, mould proliferates on every surface, birds take advantage of a shoestring roof. Emptiness leads to vacancy, which leads to desertion, and on until the state of abandonment is reached. From here, there is no more down. The stone has hit the riverbed and there it will stay: a home having been built, occupied, and finally, left.

*

Derelict houses come in two main variants: those that are merely abandoned, with no apparent cause, and those that have succumbed to fire or flood. Most are upright, some just barely. They have an uncanny habit of just appearing, fully formed and already in disrepair. I have never seen someone *abandon* a property, but I have seen what they have left behind: dank corridors, broken ceramics, bludgeoned benchtops. Anger, boredom, rage, restlessness; all were present, and all have left their mark.

An abandoned house is slow to decay. When you first encounter it, it seems solid, unwavering, like a sentinel. Then, you pass it by later, at another time, and notice the roof has depressed somewhat. Inside, the ceiling has caved to gravity's beckon, exposing the rafters, frosted and eaten by moss. The insulation, now disintegrating on the dry floor, is dressed in dirt and sopping wet.

One house, on the outskirts of town, was gutted by a particularly gluttonous fire. The fire had scorched the walls, painted them midnight; the interior furnishings were now mostly charcoal. Broken glass jutted out of window-panes, shards booby-trapping the floor. Spiders, undisturbed by humans, had celebrated each abandonment anniversary; cobwebs were everywhere, looped and hung about like streamers.

Inside felt unwelcoming, alien. Outside, the evening sun was casting an orange glow, but here all was uniformly dim. Rounding a corner into a barren hallway, the light from the doorway evaporated, subsumed by the darkness like an ocean shelf. This was no longer a space for living – what was before me was withering and silent. The house had died, and now I was standing in its corpse. Staring into the gloom, an ascending urge to retreat swam up, started tugging on my sleeve. A dog started baying outside; I took this as my cue and hastily departed.

*

Exploring an abandoned house is not without risk. There might be squatters inside; the floor may be thin; the ceiling close to collapse. I do not know how long it has been since someone was last there and, often more pressing, when they may return. Even when abandoned, a house is still private property; when I step inside, the law considers me a trespasser.

That mentioned, I do still go. Being there answers an unmet need in me. In my life, the dead have no place of visibility and often no place in conversation. I have never seen a dead body, never felt a cold hand or smelt a growing staleness. Abandoned houses offer a proxy, an important example of visible, accessible death. They are evidence, enabling a humble but muscular understanding of what happens after life leaves. This is death that I can move around in and witness, explore, and learn at my own pace. There is nothing inherently frightening about these spaces, except for the fears that you bring in with you.

I have yet to encounter anyone within a home when I have gone exploring, but the debris of their past presence is abundant. Dirty footsteps can be seen on the carpet; doors and walls are dented and smashed with fists or feet or hammers. Small metal cylinders are often found in corners, clustering like silver mushrooms. Graffiti is ubiquitous; no abandoned home is complete without it. I have seen spray-painted, Sistine-style toilets and baroque bathrooms; abstract pantries and nightmarish, postmodern kitchens. This is low art, only made by – and accessible to – the intruder. People were here, and will continue to come and go, making these spaces their transient, temporary homes until the support beams fail.

*

There is something melancholic yet, ultimately, communionable about being in a place so private and public. To step into an abandoned home is to share a moment of intimacy with those who once lived there. I return to the homes I have found; I explore to find new ones. Eventually, each of them will disappear entirely. I imagine them crumbling away as if made of sand under a midnight deluge; a slick, dark dream of undoing. One day they are there – and one day you pass by a strange space, something missing, pause, and notice they are gone.

Such homes give a glimpse into the future, a chance to look around; to learn, wonder, and find a way in. How unbearable it must be – how difficult and incredible it is, to be made, and then to be broken open. To be full of wood and copper and many little lives, sighing the long sigh until the lungs are thin and rise no more.

My Mother's Voice

Cindy Wang

When she talks there's someone cracking
glow sticks in her stomach, threading
candy through each bone of her rib cage
so the whole room lights up, scattering soft pollen
tussling on the mouths of tepid bays.
Words tingle and caper on shorelines recalling
a childhood buried in a breeze now flowing
through cities who no longer recognise her name
with stories of cherry trees
lining the sidewalk and melted crayons
on pavements chasing dragonflies that she fears
will be trampled like distorted murmurs
in the crevices of dank alleyways, gutted on chopping
boards or bulldozed into strangled sardine, but when I
watch the clockwork of her hand moulding shadow
symphonies against the fireplace,
lips drumming rain and breath spread like moonbeams
coating the city square, her voice is
a cigar lighting thunder
a voice that is Escher's hands *Drawing Hands*
drawing hands and in the foliage
of her mind I have plucked
cherry trees on the way home and tasted crayons
melting on pavements.

Why I Am Afraid

Cindy Wang

In any case, I think I'm afraid because
                                    well,
there has been a newsletter warning of
a new PHENOMENON that leaves you warped in a
spineless mass of desire, so when you say
Do you want to go to yes yes comes tumbling like
spasms of telephone wires, or cold barley tea.
'Life is about trial and error.' 'Yes,
you have to get through the bad
eggs to reach the good batch.' We were
playing hooky at my house. Turns out
I have a doctorate in studying the space
between eyelashes. This is
scaring me. You finish talking about crocodiles
and all the while I have been patiently harvesting,
cultivating something I can't name.
At the snapdragon gateway, someone has been
knocking tenaciously like a short-tempered
metronome, and who was I
to deny that? Perhaps school rules, but there are
more important things I must protect. The frozen
trains have started running again,
rippling billowing surging
even if I disagree.

Grand Final Friday

Sascha Morrell

Slipping out of the office ten minutes early, getting a seat on the 4:55 bus. Fellow passengers keeping to themselves, mostly browsing or texting or gaming on their tablets, earbuds out or in. A couple wearing dust masks because of the smoke haze. One or two maybe reading ebooks, another flipping through a printed document. Teenagers up the back leaning and breathing on each other, grungy in partial uniform but not overloud or obtrusive, unselfconsciously snapping selfies. No one checking on the world outside.

I let the side down too—I didn't even check my phone. Leaning my head against the window, I closed my eyes. I don't remember if anyone sat down beside me. I don't remember touching off.

That was Valentine's Day.

This morning I'm alone at the kitchen table with my phone, a supermarket catalogue, the grey remains of breakfast oatmeal, and the home-alone haunted feeling. I've been trying to get myself to text or email someone, or to make a gratuitous doctor's appointment, thinking it's funny how haunted I still feel in isolation, when surely the only form of haunting that can plausibly exist is having other people in our lives.

Instead of reaching for the phone, I flip to page three of the catalogue with its laundry powders and scouring pads, which make perfect sense, but when I flip over and see the improbable weekly special of tents and barbecue tongs, it tingles down my neck again: the sense that I'm the last person on earth alive.

I rise and drift to the window, and it could be true. There's no one in sight. My kitchen looks out on a strip of new townhouses, beige and slate grey, with four identical white gates like blank protest signs. They sold months ago, but no one ever comes or goes, and perhaps no one ever moved in. They cannot possibly be haunted, unless the ghosts were installed by the developers, under the floating floors.

I hold my breath for a moment, clenched against the stillness, before sliding the window open and sticking my head out to peer up and down along the street.

There's no one, left or right. There's no background noise, no birdsong. No smell of freshly mown or hosed grass or fresh dogshit or food preparation to suggest a living thing doing the business of living unseen in a hidden backyard. And if there's a breeze, I can't feel it.

Eventually, I draw back and close the window. I stand a long time with my back to the empty room, haunting my own house.

To get moving, I remind myself that I haven't been out yet today. Then I move quickly. I don't bother to think up a reason. I just grab my phone and find my wallet in my denim jacket and snatch a fresh mask from the box by the door and hurry outside.

The day is artificially warm, the sky overcast: an expired napalm glare. I don't know which way to turn at first, then I turn deliberately to the right: my old familiar five-block walk to the intersection with what passes for a main road in the inner-outer-west, where the bus runs half hourly on weekdays; where a rotating cast of the same strangers used to hop down beside me every weeknight, heading home. But it isn't familiar. Emptiness effects a quiet rearrangement of geometry, whereby the street scene at once seems larger and less three-dimensional. A stillness undisturbed by my own movement.

Still I keep moving, passing two big blonde-brick houses, their double lock-up garages frozen in time. Passing older homes—the weatherboards and bungalows, with well-tended front yards unattended. Passing the rows of green and yellow lidded wheelie bins lined up in driveways. Colorbond fences, unfenced lawns, neat garden beds with plants which seem to have ceased to photosynthesize. The drooping crucifix of a beanie bear tied to a mailbox. A concrete lion, flanked by fluorescent hydrangeas without bees. Passing underneath the one ghost gum, branches spread grey on the white sky like an upside-down map of the lungs.

Trying not to hear the silence, my breath inside the mask the only breeze. Trying to visualise the bus stop and focusing on that goal, training my eyes on the middle-distant then imminent intersection, although within two blocks of the main road, I still don't see any movement, or hear traffic. Trying to remember the timetable for Sunday and holidays, reassuring myself there'll be one before long, but fearing that when I reach the main road, there'll still be no signs of traffic, nobody waiting.

Sure enough, there's nothing. A cluster of shut-up shops, the bus shelter empty. Yet the timetable stands out bright on its pole in the grey-white glare, and when I scan the framed white printout (current date range), I see that the bus is due any minute now. *10:47.* It's 10:45.

I wait. I wait until five minutes past when the bus was due, then twelve, then until it's too late to be late, telling myself that it might have run early, but knowing if that were the case, I would have seen it from the side-road.

I fish out my phone and check the public transport app to confirm the timetable. Then I dare check my email again. Still nothing. No other messages or notifications, though there seems to be full service, because I can browse freely. The news, the web (the world) are still there. Headlines with updates on deaths and case numbers provide assurance that life goes on. I see new likes on old posts. I watch the daily Google animation. I visit random Wikipedia pages: *Black-Faced Ibis. Friends (Season 2).* I don't sit down to wait, although the narrow metal bench looks surgically sterile, and I don't remove my mask, which doesn't dig in, or even seem to grow damp with my breath. *Flood Basalt. The Second Fleet.* There are no service alerts for my route, no matter how often I hit refresh on the app or the government website. No *Expect delays.*

But after almost an hour, the road ahead still has no hum, and although I continue to wait, I'm starting to feel certain that if an empty bus ever arrives, I will not see myself reflected in its side. I will not be here, and there'll be no one else around to feel the breeze—the sigh, like a last gasp of spent air—as the houses left behind, haunted by the absence of all haunting, collapse upon themselves.

33

King Tide

Callum Methven

I

High tide gets higher every year.

Leave your full moon
    to the High Street billionaires club,
    yachts to the fading shoreline
to the underwater pier,
        leave this shrinking land to your
    children's children.

II

Low tide forgets what she used to look like.

Leave your mud
    to the crabs to the shrimp, your warming waves,
            there is a storm on her horizon,
        leave the bill to the bastards not-yet-born.

III

My mountain is an island
The trees burn skyward once a year.

We die younger die younger,
                die slowly
                die softly

    But we know deep down that this king never will.

34

Housewife III

Elizabeth Streeter

The house is a succession of blue rooms.
The unwavering matriarch is on her knees, making a
gritty paste of bicarb soda and white distilled vinegar.
She is flanked by a yellow bucket and a stout bottle of
bleach. She scrubs at the muck of critter wings and
faeces traipsed in by her children. Her son watches

her behind as she works, entranced by the long fabric of
her skirt as it dusts her ankles. Her feet are alarming: two
purpled plums for heels, fraying toenails, a sordid sketch
of cracks and divots. He prods one with his plastic train.
The woman stands and lights the burner, moving about
the kitchen as a seasoned dame should. She slips back
into her red patent

Mary Jane's – she likes wearing heels around the house.
The height, the loud echoey clunks that sound
authoritative. She kneads the package of raw chicken on
the bench, massages salt into the shiny pink thighs. She
spends several silent minutes plucking at white, fatty
globules and discarding them into the sink. Hard,

unyielding butter is applied in generous mounds to the
pocked heads of potatoes. Carrots are steamed – within

an inch of their life! The chicken is skewered
onto wooden sticks with garish, miscellaneous
vegetables. The stodgy coating of breadcrumbs and stock
is her husband's favourite.

Soon dinner is served. She calls to her feverish children.
The sodden transgression mills around the stovetop, a
perverse choir of mucus sucking and husky coughing.
She heaps their plates high and arranges her own into a
mock smiley face. Two potato eyes, a chicken nose, and
a carrot mouth. Happiness would be eating a small meal
and feeling satisfied, but her fingers are like pincers,

sneaking scraps from the children's plates when their
downy heads are turned. The day gathers itself behind
the hills and soft plinks of rain assault glass. The cheap
blinds hang like resigned arms. A measure of whiskey is
poured into a sticky tumbler and she hurries it down her
throat, a little sun in her chest.

35

Housewife IV

Elizabeth Streeter

She washes in the subdued light of the bathroom. An
orange glow blooms from the single bulb and a swarm of
midges hums muzzily around the light source. Between
her pruned lips she balances a torpid cigarette. She
smokes because her husband isn't home, and it thrills her
to let flakes of ash fall freely, peppering

the surface of the grey water. She pretends this bath is
her own, that the water has not already been sullied by
the bodies of two children. She bathes with haste,
rushing a razor along the gradient of each thigh. Each
stroke is a hushed gasp across immense plains of golden
down.

She soaps the soft skin of her belly and runs a rag under
the swell of each breast. At last she is satisfied: after
towelling herself she proceeds into the kitchen to plate
dinner. The gravy has congealed to ashen jelly in its
porcelain boat. She coaxes the marshy slop onto thick
slices of broiled beef, then arranges

the mashed potato into lopsided turrets. She makes up a
plate for her husband and stows it in the oven. Before
bed, she mixes a hot toddy for each of her children, a

sweet broth of honey, lemon, and bourbon. In her own room, she sits at the dresser and readies herself. In the small square of yellow light, she pats rouge

on her ruddy cheeks – sow's cheeks. She opens a mirrored compact and appraises the cratered rows of baked powders. She fingers the little circle of blue, using this to coat her lids. She stands to dress. The lace of her garter belt has curled and yellowed with age and her stockings are a series of flesh-coloured ladders.

To finish, she dabs cloying rosewater behind her ears and shoulders the matted plumage of her fur coat. She moves to retrieve the small case that lies in the black space under the bed, but she balks at the whisper of soles traversing the hall carpet. She slips between the cold sheets and feigns sleep.

It is only her son. He mews softly until she rolls on her side to make a narrow column of space. He climbs into the bed, pushing the length of his damp body against hers. His pants are wet through. His hot breath on her neck: she counts the seconds between each release of air. Time sedates her.

Contributors

Editors

Jessica Phillips is a PhD candidate in Literary Studies at Monash University. Her thesis examines empathy between human and nonhuman animals in contemporary Australian literature. She works as an editor in youth mental health research and her non-fiction writing has been published in *Overland*.

Anders Villani holds an MFA from the University of Michigan's Helen Zell Writers' Program, where he received the Delbanco Prize for poetry. His first full-length collection, Aril Wire, was released in 2018 by Five Islands Press. A PhD candidate in Creative Writing at Monash University, he lives in Melbourne. www.andersvillani.com.

Georgia White is a writer, editor and researcher based in Naarm/Melbourne. She is currently completing a PhD in Literary Studies, examining space, mobility and gender in eighteenth- and nineteenth-century Gothic texts. Her writing has appeared in *Australian Book Review*, *Overland* and SBS Voices, amongst others.

Authors and Artists

Eva Birch writes poetry and essays. She is also a psychoanalyst in training and completed her PhD on the work of Luce Irigaray at the University of Melbourne. Her work has appeared in min. report, *Cordite Poetry Review*, *Sick Leave*, *Codette* (NY), *Scum Mag*, *Dissect Journal*, and *Un. Magazine*, among others. *Megalodon*, her first chapbook, was published in 2019 by SOd press.

Derek Chan is a recent Creative Writing Honours graduate from Monash University. Hi swriting can be found in Australian journals such as *Cordite Poetry Review* and *Verge*.

Stacy Chan is a fourth year Arts/Law student, majoring in Literary Studies. She writes poems drawing from experiences of diaspora and romantic rebellion.

Terry Craven is a painter and co-owner of Desperate Literature book-shop, Madrid. His writing has appeared in *The London Magazine* and *3:AM Magazine* and his painting is currently being exhibited at Galería Arniches 26, Madrid.

Soumik Deb recently finished his degree in Arts. He is currently working at an engineering consultancy firm and at a cafe while he gears up for a Master's. He spent a while editing for Keith Bulfin, author of *Undercover*, and is now in the market for more editing gigs.

Joan Fleming is the author of two collections of poetry, *The Same as Yes* and *Failed Love Poems*, both from Victoria University Press, and the pamphlets *Two Dreams in Which Things Are Taken* (Duets) and *Some People's Favourites* (Desperate Literature). Recent nonfiction has been published in *Meanjin*, *Westerley*, and *The Pantograph Punch*. She holds a PhD in ethnopoetics from Monash University, and a dystopian verse novel exploring ritual and the limits of love in the ruins of ecological collapse is forthcoming with Cordite Books.

Gemma Grant is a Melbourne-based writer and student completing a Bachelor of Laws/Arts degree at Monash University. She has a particular interest in modernist fiction and looks forward to continuing her studies in creative writing. She also studies French and enjoys playing the flute in her spare time.

Rowan Heath is a fiction writer and student living on Wurundjeri land. They have a Bachelor of Arts with Honours from Monash University, and are studying a Master's degree in Publishing and Communications in 2021. They self-publish a satirical zine called *SLUMP*. They're also working on a book about small town transgender vampires, focusing on family, trauma, and LGBTIQ+ themes.

Maya Irving is a visual artist currently based on Dhudhuroa country (Beechworth). Maya works with colour and texture to convey her experience of both her inner and outer landscapes. Her work can be seen at https://www.mayairving.com.

Magdalena Kozlowski grew up in regional NSW and has been a poet all their life. Their work is informed by lived experience of chronic pain and disability, as well as a belief that words are the way to touch one another's worlds.

Callum Methven is a writer and translator from Bunyip, Australia. His poetry and short fiction have appeared in Monash University Publishing's *Verge* anthology, and he has a healthy predilection for science-fiction.

Sascha Morrell is a Sydney-born writer now based in Melbourne, where she lectures in literary studies at Monash University. Her creative writing has appeared in various Australian, British and American journals and anthologies, including *Meanjin*, *Cordite*, and *Going Down Swinging*.

Jackson C. Payne is a writer from Aotearoa-New Zealand who resides in Naarm-Melbourne. He is a doctoral candidate at Monash University, where his research is in the short story cycle. Jackson's work has appeared in *The Spinoff* and *Newsroom*, and he has a story forthcoming in *Fresh Ink*. A documentary he wrote, *Candy's Crush*, is screening at film festivals around the world. Jackson sometimes teaches creative writing.

Riya Rajesh migrated from India to Melbourne as a four-year-old and is cranky about her decrease in spice tolerance. She is an advocate of diversity and accessibility in the Arts, through proudly voicing her experiences as a woman of colour and organising community events. While she is constantly learning and unlearning, her pieces have featured in the 2020 Melbourne Spoken Word Gala, *Lot's Wife Magazine*, the *Pocketry Almanack* and more. Find her work around the city's spoken word scene and on Instagram @riyawritesincolour.

Parth Sharma is an Indian-born Kiwi writer and science student, living in Melbourne. His work strives to explore what he thinks are the overlooked and unspoken facets of life, utilising his personal experiences. He mainly writes poems. However, he's recently been spotted branching out into essay and fiction, because other forms may hold his thoughts better, and he can't make up his mind which.

Elizabeth Streeter is a Melbourne-based writer who is in her last semester of university, studying creative writing and music. She is an avid singer, walker and vegetable grower. She is currently filling her spare time writing and as a volunteer editor for *Australian Book Review*.

Shalom Verghese is a PhD researcher based in the Faculty of Arts at Monash University (Clayton). Her upcoming doctoral dissertation will focus on the representation of masculinity in popular YA fantasy fiction.

Cindy Wang is currently in her fourth year studying a double degree Bachelor of Laws and Arts. She is inspired by Frank O'Hara's spontaneous and conversational writing style, as well as Surrealism poetry and its focus on delving into the subconscious to reveal reality. In particular, Cindy is fascinated by the way in which poetry can be used to heighten, jarr and de-familiarise the sensation of images as they are perceived. In her spare time, she can be found reading coming of age novels and writing short stories.

Savanna Wegman is a Naarm based multidisciplinary artist, director and writer who draws from her fascinations with theatrical experiences, imaginative landscapes, characters and dreams. Her writing has been featured in *Flash Cove* poetry journal and is also being developed in experimental script forms.

Chen Yang was a Master's student in Creative Writing at the University of Sydney from 2019 to 2020. She is interested in writing poetry and prose.

Gavin Yates is a writer and researcher. His poetry has been published in *Cordite Poetry Review*, *Island Magazine*, *Southerly* and *Westerly*.

CPSIA information can be obtained
at www.ICGtesting.com
Printed in the USA
LVHW081149050921
696831LV00007B/13

9 781922 464439